This book belongs to

_____

_____

_____

To Antonieta
and all my best friends
that are crazy for music,
like me.

Tales from the Hidden Valley: The Band is © Flying Eye Books 2019.

This is a first edition published in 2019 by Flying Eye Books,
an imprint of Nobrow Ltd. 27 Westgate Street, London, E8 3RL.

Text and illustrations © Carles Porta 2019.

1 3 5 7 9 10 8 6 4 2

Translation © Lawrence Schimel.

Published in the US by Nobrow (US) Inc.

Printed in Latvia on FSC ® certified paper.

ISBN: 978-1-911171-67-6

www.flyingeyebooks.com

Tales from the Hidden Valley

The Band

Carles Porta

Flying Eye Books

London | New York

Hidden far away between tall mountains, there lies a secret valley. You could pass it a hundred times and still not see it, unless you knew just where to look...

The melting snow rushed down from the mountain peaks as the sun began to shine. The silence of winter disappeared as the sounds of birds echoed throughout the valley. Spring had finally arrived.

After a long journey, Ticky reached his nest at
the top of the Dead Tree. With a bit of sweeping,
it would once more be the cosiest of places,
with the best views of the valley.

In the apartment below, Maximilian Cold played
a loud TUT-FANT-BLURT on his trumpet as he'd
done every morning since moving into the tree.

Upstairs, Ticky's heart nearly burst from his chest.
What a surprise! It seemed he had a new neighbour
– one who played the trumpet.

Just then came the sound of a band. Marching across the fields was Sara playing the drums, the Morten brothers playing their home-made instruments and Yula playing her blue ukelele.

Ticky watched them from his window, filled with joy. His friends were coming to welcome him home! He was just about to jump down and give them all a hug, when...

...one by one, his friends disappeared into
the trunk, without even saying hello to him.

Ticky felt the world falling in on him. What were they
doing down there? Had they forgotten him already?

Inside Max's home, Ticky's friends hadn't realised he had arrived home early. They were too busy organising a secret party for him.

Max suggested rehearsing a song to welcome Ticky, when suddenly his body began to move in a surprising way.

His head started bobbing, and his legs made
such tall leaps he had to leave the house!

That spring morning, the music made
him feel as if he was as light as a feather.

"Things have changed a lot here,"
Ticky thought, as he gloomily watched
everyone following his new neighbour,
the trumpeter.

Ticky seemed to have become invisible.

Leading the band, Max danced over streams and strode through reeds. His trumpet echoed from one side of the valley to the other.

Ana, the gardener fairy, who was always very
busy in springtime, looked up from her work.

She grabbed her flute and went in search
of the sound, passing Ticky along the way.

Meanwhile, Max skipped over enormous water lilies.
On hearing the music, insects large and small,
birds, worms, frogs, fairies, pixies and all kinds of living
creatures followed him.

Feeling blue, Ticky sat by the river. Just then,
he saw Onion-head drift past, and without
thinking twice, decided to join her.

Riding on a log, the pair let themselves
be carried on the current. Silence and
darkness surrounded them...

Ogre, as usual, was in a very bad mood. He had spent all morning fishing without any luck.

The last thing he imagined to catch in the river was a blue bird!

But, it was better than nothing at all ... and he was very hungry.

Ticky thought the day was getting worse.
He would surely be made into pie!

But just then, in the distance,
he heard a TOOT TOOT!

Meanwhile, Maximilian had continued dancing and trumpeting right into a dark forest full of strange trees.

The rest of the band froze as they watched him disappear into the shadows. Everyone except Max knew that the path led right to Ogre's cabin!

Soon, even the sound of his trumpet faded away.

Yula was so worried she ran straight into
the forest. She had to save Max from his fate!

Without thinking, Sara followed her and then all the others ran after them both, weaving over vines and creeping under canopies. The Dark Forest had never been so lively!

Nearing closer, they could hear the sound of Max's trumpet again. Although, was that a violin they could hear too?

Deep in the forest, they found Ogre and Max dancing together like crazy. What a relief! But the party didn't last long...

Yula discovered that Ticky was being kept as prisoner in a nearby tree. How awful!

Ogre was so ashamed of himself that he agreed to let him go.

Once certain that Ticky was safe, Yula crept
up to Sara and whispered an idea into her ear.

Whilst Yula and Ticky walked home, the others
began sneaking back to Max's apartment...

Sprinting towards the Dead Tree, over the same
vines and under the same canopies, the gang ran.
They had to finish preparing Ticky's surprise party!

Arriving at his beloved Dead Tree, Ticky felt moved.
"It really is the best home in the world," he smiled.
Ticky laughed as he remembered he now had a loony
neighbour who played the trumpet very well.

Entering the front door, Ticky jumped so high
he nearly hit the clouds. What a surprise!
So this is what his friends had been planning!

The party would be remembered in the valley for a long
time. And without realising, summer arrived, bringing with
it plenty more memories ... but that's for another story.